Shiver Me Letters

A Pirate
A B C

SHIVER ME LETTERS

A PIRATE ABC

June Sobel   Illustrated by Henry Cole

sandpiper

Houghton Mifflin Harcourt

Boston   New York

The illustrations in this book were done in watercolor and ink
on Arches hot press watercolor paper.
The display type was set in Belwe. The text type was set in P22 1722.

SANDPIPER and the SANDPIPER logo are trademarks of Houghton Mifflin Harcourt Publishing Company.

The Library of Congress has cataloged the hardcover edition as follows:
Sobel, June.
Shiver me letters: a pirate ABC/written by June Sobel; illustrated by Henry Cole.
p. cm.
Summary: Having decided that R is not enough for them, a bumbling
band of pirates sets sail on a quest to capture the rest of the alphabet.
[1. Pirates—Fiction.   2. Alphabet—Fiction.   3. Stories in rhyme.]
I. Cole, Henry, 1955- ill. II. Title.
PZ8.3.S692Sh 2006
[E]—dc22   2005008902
ISBN: 978-0-15-216732-5 ISBN: 978-0-15-206679-6 pb

Manufactured in China

SCP   15 14 13 12 11

4500577274

To my own pirates,
Mark and Adam R.
— J. S.

With love to Penoir
and Nancoir, my own
little Aruban pirate crew
— H. C.

"R," cried the crew.
"R, we agree!
Let's look for an A and
a B and a C!"

They set up their sails
and followed the wind.
Spying an island,
they toothlessly
grinned.

"Land ho!"
yelled the pirates
as they rowed to the west.
"Capture those letters.
Let's make it our quest!"

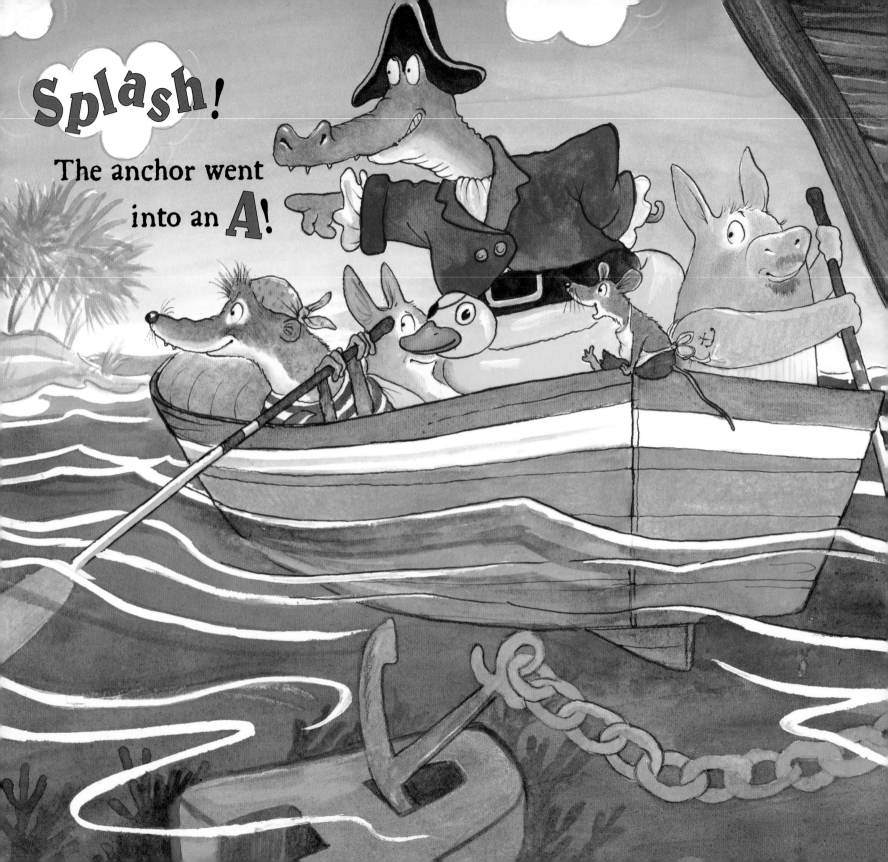

Splash!

The anchor went into an A!

A **B** floated by on
the crystal clear bay.

In a chest glistened **G**,
all shiny and gold.

H hung from the hook
on a pirate of old.

Ten paces north
stood a huge ivory I.

From out of the jungle, J jumped sky-high.

A **K** on a key slid under a shell.

Far from the water hid landlubber **L**.

A mysterious map with an **M** soon appeared,

while one nimble **N** popped right out of a beard!

They soon spotted **O** rolling into the ocean.

A parrot squawked, "P!"
What a commotion!

The gang questioned **Q** as it quacked in its nest.

"**R**," cried the crew. "When do we rest?"

They saw **S** in the shape
of a swashbuckling sword,

then found **T** on a turtle as they hauled him aboard.

The crew dove underwater, caught **U** in a net.

They viewed **V** veiled in velvet, all soaking wet.

A wave washed up , sunburned and hot.

Pirates explored to find **X** marked the spot!

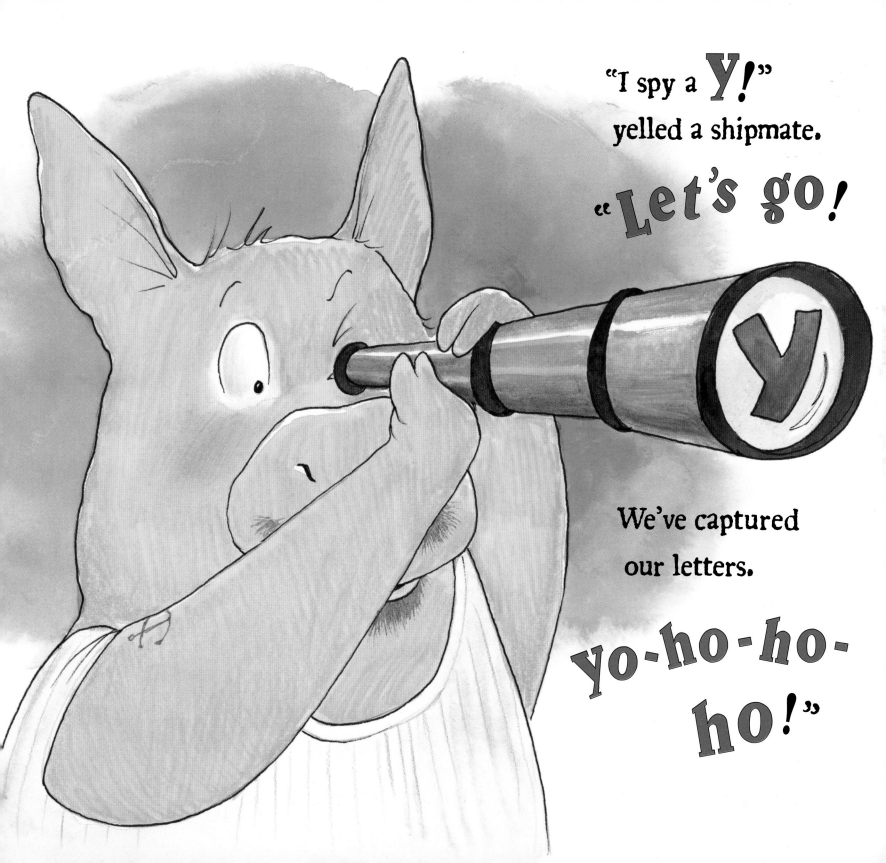

They went to the captain
expecting a thanks.
They showed him the letters.
He showed them the planks.

"**R**," cried the crew. "Our work is not done.

We'll search and we'll plunder
to find the last one!"

And that very night
as they snored in their beds,
zillions of **Z**'s zoomed all over their heads.